THE

Miracle Man

Other X-Files books in this series

Prologue

The town of Kenwood, Tennessee, hadn't seen this much excitement in years. Not since Elvis had driven through in his pink Cadillac, thirty years earlier.

Elvis had made it.

This Caddy hadn't.

Speeding, it had swerved to miss another car, bounced off a van, and hit a telephone pole. Then it burst into flames.

Now Kenwood's usually sleepy Main Street was littered with broken glass and twisted steel, and jammed with fire trucks, police cars, and ambulances. State troopers held back a crowd of curious onlookers, drawn from nearby houses and late-night cafés by the crash.

The darkness was lit by the *whoosh* of

flames as the Cadillac's gas tank exploded.

The crowd that had gathered backed up in horror. "The driver's still in there!" someone yelled.

The crowd pressed forward again as the flames died down. The state troopers pressed them back as two firemen ran toward the Cadillac with a powerful saw and a hydraulic "jaws of life" machine. Two paramedics followed with a gurney.

There was a screech of metal and a crack as the door was popped off the Cadillac. The blackened body that the paramedics pulled out was clearly finished.

No one even bothered to check for a pulse.

The dead man was zipped into a black plastic body bag.

The crowd watched it all with silent curiosity.

Then a middle-aged man in a dark suit and a ten-year-old boy pushed to the front of the crowd.

"It's that tent preacher," someone whispered.

"Excuse me," said the man. "Let us through, please, thank you . . ."

The crowd parted like the Red Sea. This was the Bible Belt, where preachers were respected.

Paramedics wheeled the gurney with the body bag toward a waiting ambulance.

The fire chief flagged them down. "What's going on?" he shouted.

"This one's dead," said a paramedic.

The chief pointed toward the van, crumpled against the curb across the street.

One dazed passenger was throwing up alongside the road. Another was lying on the street, gasping for breath.

"Well, there's a woman over there who isn't dead," the chief told him. "And she needs some oxygen!"

"Yes, sir!"

Leaving the gurney in the middle of the street, the paramedics headed for the van.

"More water! Over there!"

The chief was giving orders to his firemen,

who were dousing the last of the flames inside the Cadillac.

He didn't see the preacher and the boy duck through the police line and approach the gurney.

The preacher unzipped the body bag.

The charred thing inside no longer had a human face. It had been burned beyond recognition. Choking back nausea, the preacher turned away.

The sight didn't seem to bother the boy, though. He reached into the body bag and laid his hands on the brow of the burned head. He then closed his eyes and began to speak in a high, squeaky child's voice. It was somewhere between a prayer and a command.

"I want you to rise!" he proclaimed. "Rise up and be healed!"

A rustle of nervous laughter went through the crowd. They couldn't believe what they were seeing. This weird kid, touching a dead body. Hollering at it . . .

The fire chief looked around and saw the

preacher and the boy. He saw the boy's hands inside the body bag.

"What the hell are you doing?" he demanded.

"The boy is laying on hands," said the preacher. He spoke with a Southern drawl with a backwoods twang.

"Rise up!" the boy cried out, his voice quivering with excitement. "Accept the miracle He has given you, and forsake Him not."

The crowd stopped laughing and grew quiet. A few people pushed forward to see what would happen.

"You don't understand," said the chief. He spoke to the preacher in a calm, deliberate voice, as if he were explaining something to a child. "This man is *dead*."

"Then the boy can't possibly do any harm, can he?" the preacher asked.

Shaking his head with disgust, the fire chief turned away. No point getting into a fight with a preacher, not with a crowd looking on. These people took their religion seriously.

"For this is the power of belief," the boy was saying. "The power to separate the light from the darkness. To create life from death . . . "

The chief had heard enough. He vented his frustration on the crowd. "All right, everybody!" he shouted, waving his arms. "Show's over! Let's clear the area."

The crowd moved back slowly. Reluctantly.

Suddenly, a gasp—and the crowd stopped backing up.

The fire chief looked behind him.

A hand was rising out of the body bag. A crisp, burned, blackened hand.

The hand reached for the boy—and the boy took the gnarled, twisted fingers in his own.

"Hallelujah, Samuel!" cried the preacher. His eyes were shining with tears.

A few amens were murmured in the crowd as people shook their heads in wonder and amazement.

The boy was grinning in triumph.

Chapter One

The crowd gathered inside the large meeting tent was rocking.

The drums played a steady backbeat, the organ wailed, the people clapped and shouted.

The TV camera moved among them, picking up happy faces, swaying bodies, clapping hands.

"Hallelujah!" they called out.

They were dressed in leisure suits and discount-store jeans, bib overalls and Sunday dresses, cowboy hats and sunbonnets. They were black and white, young and old, male and female. They were the sinners and the born again. Some had wheelchairs, others had crutches, some came carrying canes. They were the salt of the earth.

They all shared one faith and one hope—that they would be healed.

The reverend urged them on, rapping into his microphone with a rich Southern accent:

"The POWER and glory of GOD are here with us TONIGHT!" he extolled.

Every third or fourth word was a shout, as high and sharp as the bark of a dog. The cadence was hypnotic, and the people responded by swaying from side to side.

"I can FEEL the miraculous PRESENCE here with me on STAGE!" the reverend shouted. He wore a dark blue suit, with white shoes and slicked-back hair. He looked much the same as he had eleven years earlier, when he had slipped his son through police lines at the scene of a fatal wreck.

His son, however, looked a great deal different. He was older, now a young man with dark, brooding eyes.

And he was as quiet as his father was loud.

"His wondrous, holy POWER is focused on his CHILDREN!" the preacher proclaimed. "Who have GATHERED here to have their

FAITH renewed and their sickness HEALED!"

While his father preached, the teenage boy approached a table where an elderly woman lay half-covered with a sheet, almost like a corpse. He was reaching out to touch her when he—*FROZE!*

Special Agent Dana Scully had just hit the Pause button on the VCR.

The two agents were in Mulder's office in the basement of the FBI building in Washington, D.C.

"This is a video of a faith-healing tent meeting in Tennessee," Scully explained. "The woman on the table has a malignant tumor on her spine."

Mulder was silent. He sat behind his desk with his feet up, watching. Scully had brought in the video and popped it into his VCR.

"The boy here"— Scully pointed to the teenager paused on the flickering screen— "is going to attempt to cure the woman by simply laying his hands on her."

"Where'd you get this?" Mulder asked.

"It came in from the regional FBI office in

Memphis," Scully told him. "The preacher's name is . . ."

"Reverend Calvin Hartley," said Mulder.

Scully turned, surprised. "You've heard of him?"

Mulder nodded, pleased as always when he could surprise his colleague. "The young man is his adopted son, Samuel. The preacher claims to have found him as an infant, lying in the tall weeds on the bank of the muddy Mississippi."

"Did you know that he claims the boy once brought a man back from the dead?"

"It's more than just a claim," Mulder asserted. "The man he saved appears as a regular attraction in the preacher's tent ministry. The boy's been performing miracles every week for the past ten years. Twice on Sunday."

Scully rolled her eyes. "They're not miracles," she told him. "At least not according to the Kenwood County sheriff. Local authorities think Hartley and his son are running a scam. They've been trying to shut him down for a while, without much luck."

"So they're coming to us?" Mulder asked.

Scully nodded. "They've turned to the FBI to try and get a prosecution."

Mulder looked surprised. "On what charge—fraud?"

Now it was Scully's turn to enjoy surprising Mulder. "No. Murder. Watch the tape."

She clicked the Play button, and the TV suddenly came back to life as young Samuel Hartley laid his hands gently on the brow of the old woman on the table.

She smiled tentatively up at the handsome young man. Her eyes were filled with fear— and hope.

Samuel smiled down at her. His dark eyes were filled with tenderness and faith. He took her hands in his and squeezed them.

Then Reverend Hartley stepped into the picture, holding his wireless microphone like a magic wand.

"Lucy Kelly has the CANCER!" Hartley declaimed.

"Her doctors call it INOPERABLE. They say it is INCURABLE. What they mean is, THEY can't cure it," he shouted.

"Amen!" responded the crowd.

Samuel put his hands on Lucy Kelly's shoulders.

"But you know what I say?" Reverend Hartley asked the crowd. "I say that what the DOCTORS cannot heal, the LORD can!"

"Hallelujah," murmured the crowd. Then louder: "HALLELUJAH!" Their voices re-sounded like the triumphant baying of a great beast awakened.

"Because GOD can work MIRACLES! And GOD'S HEALING love is FLOWING through Samuel's healing HANDS!"

Samuel's hands jerked suddenly. He pulled them away from the woman, as if they were burning.

Scully turned off the VCR. She had seen enough.

Mulder's eyes were still glued to the TV screen.

"Twenty minutes later," Scully remarked, "Lucy Kelly was taken to the hospital."

"And?"

"DOA," Scully said, indicating that the old woman was dead before the ambulance reached the hospital.

Mulder stepped behind his desk again and sat down in his chair. "What was the cause of death?"

"They don't know," Scully replied. "But it wasn't cancer."

She turned to face Mulder. He sat quietly with his feet on his desk.

"They've requested someone with a medical background to assist the local police on the investigation," Scully said. "I know this isn't an X-File, but—"

Mulder interrupted her. "When do we leave for Tennessee?"

Chapter Two

"Step right up, folks! The service is about to begin!"

People were hurrying out of their cars, streaming into the tent that baked under the hot Tennessee sun.

The sign over the entrance read:

REVEREND CALVIN HARTLEY PRESENTS HIS

MIRACLE MINISTRY

FEATURING HEALER SAMUEL HARTLEY

COME AS YOU ARE . . .

LEAVE AS YOU ALWAYS WANTED TO BE!

Scully and Mulder stood together at the entrance to the tent, under the sign. They looked out of place in their city shoes and conservative suits.

The people streaming into the tent were the same sort of folks they had seen in the video: all shapes and sizes, colors, sexes, and ages. They were dressed informally, in jeans, casual outfits, and work clothes.

Mulder was more interested in the vendors than in the outfits. Tables on either side of the entrance to the tent were selling T-shirts, programs, "sanctified" vials of creek water, and envelopes filled with dirt—relics of all the people young Samuel Hartley had healed.

Supposedly healed.

"Can you believe this?" Mulder muttered to Scully as he turned over a small framed photo of the "miracle boy." He looked around at the crowd streaming past. "I think I saw some of these same people at Woodstock."

Scully smiled wryly. "Mulder, you weren't at Woodstock."

"I saw the movie," Mulder confessed as he pulled two tickets from the breast pocket of his gray suit and showed them at the door.

They were both surprised and pleased to

find that the inside of the tent was cool.

"Air-conditioned," sighed Scully. "Like heaven."

"Or," whispered Mulder, "the better parts of hell."

In back of the rapidly filling tent, a van pulled into a parking space marked "Handicapped." The van's license plate showed the wheelchair symbol.

Sheriff Maurice Daniels got out and walked around the van to the passenger window, where his wife waited patiently.

"This shouldn't take too long, Lillian," Daniels said. "Will you be all right here by yourself?"

"I'll be fine," she assured him, smiling bravely.

"I won't be long." Sheriff Daniels nodded and patted her hand. Then he joined the throng streaming into the tent.

Lillian Daniels watched, her eyes filled with pain. Her crippled arthritic fingers gripped the window of the van.

She longed to join the crowd, but she couldn't.

Her husband didn't believe. And he wouldn't allow her to believe either.

Mulder and Scully found two chairs in the back row and sat down.

Even though people were still coming in, making noise as they looked for seats and greeted their neighbors, Reverend Hartley's voice started booming through the tent, amplified by giant speakers flanking the stage.

"MOST of you here TODAY I know as NEIGHBORS," he proclaimed. "CHERISHED members of our MIRACLE Ministry!"

Scully leaned forward, straining to see.

Reverend Hartley stood on a stage that looked like the runway for a fashion show. He wore an expensive suit. His fingers flashed with rings.

"But SOME of you have COME from far away. As FAR away as PENSACOLA, Florida," he continued. "And UNIONDALE, Long Island!"

His voice rose and fell as he picked up the rhythm.

Mulder's eyes flicked over the crowd. If you had asked him what he was looking for, he couldn't have told you. It was instinct: he was gathering information that he would process and use later.

"And it is ESPECIALLY to those of you who've come so FAR that I must APOLO-GIZE from the bottom of my heart . . .

". . . because unfortunately SAMUEL cannot be here this afternoon."

Mulder and Scully looked at each other, both of them wondering what was going on here.

A low murmur of disappointment swept through the crowd.

Reverend Hartley raised his hands. His rings sparkled under the stage lights.

"I know! I know how very deeply disap-pointed each of you must be feeling right now. But I say unto you, do not be DISMAYED! Do not DESPAIR. Do not lose your hope."

Hartley's voice rose again into its hypnotic cadence: "Because in TWO short days SAMUEL will be back at our VERY special Miracle Mission." The crowd cheered loudly.

He turned and gestured behind him, and for the first time Scully and Mulder noticed the other people on the stage. Some were in wheelchairs, some on crutches. One was wearing all black—suit, hat, sunglasses, and gloves.

All were smiling, except for the man in black.

"He will be back here to work MIRACLES on the faithful, because as these folks up here are about to testify . . . Samuel can HEAL you! Samuel WILL heal you! But . . ."

Reverend Hartley paused for effect.

"Only if you BELIEVE!"

Scully had heard enough. "Maybe we should head backstage," she whispered to Mulder. "See what the reverend can tell us."

Mulder caught her arm. "Wait!"

"For what?"

"This is the part where they bring out Elvis."

Despite herself, Scully had to smile.

A few minutes later, Mulder and Scully flashed their FBI badges at Reverend Hartley as he walked out the backstage entrance to the tent and headed toward a waiting Cadillac.

"Reverend Hartley?" Scully asked, catching up with him. "We're with the FBI."

Hartley nodded, but kept walking.

Mulder fell in step beside him.

"I see Sheriff Daniels has called in the cavalry," Hartley said, looking straight ahead.

"We just want a word with Samuel," Scully informed him. "That's all."

"Well, he's not here," Hartley told her. He had reached his car and was about to get in. A man in black held the door for him.

"Where is he?" Mulder wanted to know.

Reverend Hartley paused, his hand on the car door. For the first time he looked directly at the two agents.

"I don't know," he replied. "I haven't seen him." His voice dropped. Without the cadences, it sounded almost sincere. "The boy's been a bit . . . troubled lately."

"Reverend, we're running behind," urged the man in black. His eyes were shaded by a wide hat and hidden behind dark glasses. His face was scarred and pale—as white as the belly of a dead fish.

Mulder recognized him as the man in black who had stood on stage behind Reverend Hartley.

"If you'll excuse me."

"Yes, Leonard," Hartley agreed. Nodding politely, if curtly, toward Mulder and Scully, the preacher climbed into the backseat of the limousine.

Pausing only to glare at Mulder and Scully, the man in black then got in next to the reverend.

Both doors slammed, and the limousine driver sped away.

"Agent Mulder?" asked an unfamiliar voice. Mulder and Scully turned and saw a man in uniform approaching.

He carried a manila envelope in one hand. He stuck out the other. "I'm Sheriff Daniels. We spoke on the phone."

"Right," said Mulder, shaking his hand. "I'm Mulder, and this is Agent Scully."

Daniels looked at Scully with new interest. "You're the medical doctor. You requested a copy of the coroner's reports."

"That's right."

He handed her the manila envelope.

"Thanks," she said. Scully opened it immediately and started leafing through the contents: forms, photos, X rays. All evidence of the deaths that had been linked to the Miracle Ministry.

"I see you folks got a chance to take in the Holy Roller sideshow," Sheriff Daniels said wryly, gesturing toward the Miracle Ministry tent.

"Something tells me you're not a member of Reverend Hartley's flock," Mulder surmised.

Sheriff Daniels shook his head and spat. "I remember Hartley when he was a soapbox preacher, collecting dollar bills in coffee cans.

Since the boy's joined the act, Hartley's got himself a Cadillac for every day of the week. Bought with money we should be using to improve our schools and our roads."

Mulder shrugged. "People want to believe."

Daniels spat again. "Ninety-nine percent of the people in this world are fools," he went on. "And the remaining one percent is in great danger of contagion."

The crowd had thinned. Mulder, Scully, and the sheriff started across the lawn toward the main parking lot.

"Even if Reverend Hartley and Samuel are fakes," Mulder contended, "that's still a long way from accusing them of murder."

The sheriff shook his head.

"I got witnesses who'll tell you the boy was right there, laying hands on these people when they died."

"Is that how you think he killed them?" Mulder inquired in a deliberately neutral tone. "With a touch?"

"I don't claim anything," Daniels told him. "I don't know how or why he did it. But we've been looking for the boy since Tuesday. And he does not want to be found."

"These reports indicate nothing out of the ordinary," Scully noted, handing the envelope back to Sheriff Daniels. "Except that no autopsies were performed."

"That's Hartley's doing," Sheriff Daniels reported. "He managed to block my autopsy request on religious grounds. And it doesn't help that the county coroner is a dues-paying member of the so-called Miracle Ministry."

Mulder looked at Scully, who nodded, just slightly.

"Maybe with the help of a federal warrant," Mulder said, "we could arrange to have the bodies exhumed."

For the first time Sheriff Daniels smiled. "Not a bad idea," he agreed.

Chapter Three

There is nothing so loud as a noise in a cemetery at night.

This was a rough, rude noise, echoing through the mist that swirled around the gravestones. It was a snorting, grating, racketing noise. The diesel sound of a great beast scraping into the clay.

"Can we get a little more light?" called out the bored voice of a cemetery worker.

Sheriff Daniels reached through the window of his car and turned on the headlights. Now the beast itself could be seen, lurching up and down in the mist.

The great beast was a backhoe—a hydraulic shovel mounted onto the rear of a tractor, digging a square hole at the foot of a new gravestone.

Mulder and Scully stood by the sheriff's cruiser, watching, along with Sheriff Daniels.

The gravestone belonged to one of the two recent deaths connected with Reverend Hartley's Miracle Ministry. In the eerie light, Scully could read the words carved into the stone cross:

CAROL WALLACE
"HOW DESOLATE OUR HOME
BEREFT OF THEE"
1942–1997

Mulder, as usual, was looking around, scanning the scene. He was, therefore, the first to see something approaching through the mist, down the long hill studded with gravestones.

He nudged Sheriff Daniels.

"Sheriff—"

Daniels turned, following Mulder's nod, and looked up the hillside toward the cemetery entrance.

"Damn!" he muttered.

Over the hill they came, shapes in the fog like wandering spirits. As they drew closer they resolved into human figures. Two dozen people, their faces lighted by the candles they carried cupped in their hands.

They were black and white, young and old, men and women, just as at the tent meeting. Only they were no longer shouting "hallelujah" and smiling hopefully.

They were silent, their faces grim with determination—and something that looked very much like hatred.

"That's Reverend Hartley's group," groaned Sheriff Daniels.

"How'd they find out we were here?" Scully wondered.

Sheriff Daniels shook his head ruefully. "I told my people to keep quiet so this wouldn't happen."

"Looks like you may have a few believers on your payroll," Mulder cautioned him.

Instead of answering Mulder, Sheriff

Daniels signaled to the backhoe operator by drawing his finger across his neck, meaning "shut it down."

The backhoe operator killed the engine.

The graveyard was suddenly quiet. The silence fell like a blanket. Only the crickets could be heard, like a macabre choir, as the candle-holding crowd surrounded the newly opened grave.

The man leading them was Leonard Vance. He carried a cane and walked with a limp. He wore a black hat and gloves. Dark glasses covered his eyes.

"On behalf of the Miracle Ministry," Vance intoned, "we demand that you stop this sacrilege!"

"You're not just dealing with me anymore, Vance," the sheriff responded. He nodded toward Mulder and Scully. "You're dealing with the FBI."

Scully stepped between the two men.

"We don't mean you any disrespect," she said to Vance. "We're investigating a possible homicide."

She waited, but there was no response from Vance. Scully went on: "Federal law requires that we conduct a postmortem examination of these bodies."

What was left of Vance's thin lips parted in a mocking smile. "I'm afraid we answer to a higher authority than the U.S. government. One that considers grave robbing and defiling corpses to be sins. Mortal sins."

Sheriff Daniels spat scornfully. He was about to answer when he was interrupted by a burst of static from the car radio.

He turned to answer it, shooting a hard look over his shoulder. "We'll get the autopsy, Vance. Sooner or later. You know we will!"

Then he slammed the door, grabbing the receiver: "Daniels here . . ."

Leonard Vance turned the blank gaze of his dark glasses onto the two FBI agents. "The family of the deceased does not want her grave disturbed."

Sheriff Daniels turned around. "You know damn well that Carol Wallace had no family!"

"We were her family," said Vance. With his

cane, he pointed toward the silent figures gathered around the grave. Ignoring the sheriff, he spoke directly to Mulder and Scully. "We were her family, and it was hard enough to bury her once."

Mulder looked at his partner, then looked at the silent crowd surrounding the open grave. He and Scully had the legal authority to order these people away. But did they have the means—or the will—to enforce it?

"If you insist on going through with this outrage," Vance continued, "we're prepared to maintain a vigil and do whatever it takes to stop you."

As he spoke, the crowd moved closer to the open grave, their feet shuffling through the loose clay and gravel.

Mulder was surveying the situation, deciding what course of action to take, when his thoughts were interrupted by Sheriff Daniels.

"Mulder, Scully." Daniels called them over to where he was standing.

"One of my deputies spotted the boy's car

downtown," he told them. "That's what the radio call was about."

Mulder and Scully glanced at each other with relief. This at least solved the immediate problem.

"Well, we can't do much here anyway," said Scully as she and Mulder moved away from the grave.

With a last look at the crowd by the grave, they got into the car.

Chapter Four

In every small Southern river town, no matter how small, there is one street that feels like a big city.

Gritty and mean.

One street with neon lights and no picket fences. One street with pawnshops instead of churches, cheap hotels instead of homes, honky-tonks instead of schools.

Eddie's Riverfront Bar & Grill was on that street in Kenwood, Tennessee.

The tiny parking lot at Eddie's was nearly empty. One pickup truck, one battered old "sharecropper Chevy," and one plum-colored Cadillac.

Lights flashing, the Kenwood County sheriff's cruiser pulled in, followed by a nondescript gray rental car.

The sheriff and his deputy got out of the cruiser. Mulder and Scully got out of the rental car.

"Not the most likely place to be saving souls," Sheriff Daniels quipped.

Mulder shrugged. It seemed to him like a place where there might be a few souls that needed saving.

But he kept his mouth shut. That was one thing Mulder had learned as an FBI agent. It was always tricky dealing with local authorities. And with Daniels, it seemed even trickier than usual.

The inside of the bar was a mess.

A cook in an apron was sweeping up broken glass. The bartender was straightening stools and chairs that had been knocked over.

The mirror behind the bar had been smashed. Three men stood at the bar. But they quickly finished their beers and slipped out the door when the sheriff and his deputy came in.

Sheriff Daniels walked straight up to the

bartender. "Where's the boy?" he demanded.

The bartender answered without looking up from his dustpan filled with amber fragments of glass.

"In the can."

"What happened here?" Mulder asked.

The bartender shrugged.

"Some damn fool started a fight," he grumbled. He looked toward the rear of the bar. "Figured a Bible thumper wouldn't know how to hold his liquor."

Mulder and Scully followed the bartender's glance. The men's room door swung open and Samuel Hartley staggered out.

The teenager's handsome face was battered and bloodied. He had one black eye and a cut on his cheek. But his hair was neatly combed and his shirt tucked in.

Samuel Hartley sat down at a table and lit a cigarette. He didn't seem to notice the sheriff and the two agents—or if he did notice, he didn't seem to care.

Sheriff Daniels crossed the floor and stood

over the young man. Mulder and Scully followed a few steps behind.

"Where have you been, Samuel?" the sheriff began. "I've been looking for you."

"Yeah?" Samuel took a long drag off his cigarette. He looked up at the sheriff and scowled. "I've been thinking."

"Thinking." The sheriff nodded. "You're going to have plenty of time for that, son. I'm placing you under arrest."

Mulder and Scully were both surprised to notice that the young man seemed relieved.

He took another pull of his cigarette. "For murder?"

The sheriff nodded. "Suspicion of murder."

Samuel seemed to consider this for a moment. Then he nodded. "Mind if I finish my beer first?"

"You go right on ahead," said the sheriff. "I'll be wanting to get a statement. And I'll see what I can do about getting your Caddy towed."

Daniels walked away. Mulder and Scully

followed him. "What evidence do you have to charge him with murder?" Mulder asked softly.

Sheriff Daniels stopped. He looked from Mulder to Scully, and back to Mulder.

"What more would you like?" the sheriff asked. "The boy's practically giving himself up!"

"Look at him, he's drunk," Mulder reminded him.

"So, I'll add drunk and disorderly to the charge," the sheriff said sarcastically. "Let's just get this straight. The question is not about the boy's guilt. Just how he did it."

Mulder was careful not to show any response. "Let us have a minute with him."

"Suit yourself," said Daniels, and stalked off angrily. He had asked for help from the FBI.

But so far, all he was getting was interference.

Mulder and Scully sat down at the table where Samuel was smoking his cigarette.

"I'm Special Agent Mulder. This is Agent Scully. We're with—"

"I know," Samuel interrupted. "The FBI."

"Looks like you took quite a beating," said Mulder.

Samuel touched his black eye and winced. "Penance, Mr. Mulder."

"Some might call it a plain old bar brawl," Scully remarked.

Samuel looked at her sharply. "You know what they say: He giveth and He taketh away."

"Meaning?"

Samuel shrugged. "A man gets too proud, sometimes it does him good to get the crap kicked out of him. Pardon my language."

Scully nodded.

"Saves God the trouble," he added.

"Trouble of what?" asked Scully.

Samuel took another drag off his cigarette. "Humbling the guilty sinner."

"Guilty of what?" she persisted.

Mulder was more explicit. "Guilty of murder?"

Samuel looked down. "Yes, sir," he said in a low voice.

Mulder looked dubious and interested at the same time. "How'd you do it, Samuel?"

"Apparently my pride and weakness were an invitation to the devil. I muddied the water of my own faith. My gift has been corrupted," Samuel declared.

"Wait a minute," Scully interjected. "So you're saying you killed those people by just touching them?"

Samuel Hartley's eyes blazed with a new intensity. "I've laid my hands on the ill and given them health. I've healed the sick. I've even touched the dead and given them life. God gave me a special gift."

Scully allowed herself a slight, wry smile. "Did God buy you all of that jewelry, too?" she said, indicating his hands, which glittered with rings. "Maybe there's a part of the story you're leaving out."

Samuel looked injured. He stubbed out his cigarette and clenched his hands into fists. His eyes were fierce, his voice now raised.

"You doubt the power of God, ma'am?"

"No," Scully replied. "Just the veracity of your claims."

The intensity returned to Samuel's eyes. Scully was fascinated. It was as if a light had come on in an empty house. "I can look on the infirm and see their sickness, their cancer," he told her. "I can look into the windows of their souls. Just as I can look on this man here and see his pain, deep inside."

Mulder glanced around to make sure Samuel was talking about him.

Apparently so.

"Really," Mulder exclaimed, his voice heavy with irony. "And what pain is that?"

Samuel Hartley's voice was soft again. He avoided the agents' eyes. "The pain you have regarding a brother. Or a sister."

Mulder looked up sharply.

"It's an old pain," said Samuel. "One that has never healed."

Mulder's poker face was gone. He tried to hide his reaction with a smirk.

Scully noticed, though. She didn't like it.

"Is this some kind of a trick?" she asked Samuel.

Samuel looked her straight in the eye. "No trick, ma'am."

Scully rose from her chair. It was time to terminate the interview. "I think we should let the sheriff take over."

Mulder caught her arm. "No. Wait."

He turned to Samuel. "I want to hear this. About the pain. Tell me."

Samuel closed his eyes. He spoke quietly. All his former passion was gone, and he spoke like a robot—or a man possessed.

"I can see it. Plain as day. It's a sister. You lost a sister. Quite young. Too young. Someone took her—away."

Mulder's face was impassive, but the trembling of his hands revealed his feelings.

Scully beckoned to Sheriff Daniels. She wanted some help.

"What else?" Mulder demanded, all his attention focused on the teenager. "What else do you see?"

"Strangers. A bright light."

Scully was getting desperate. "Sheriff Daniels!" she called out.

Samuel opened his eyes and fixed them on Mulder. They were filled with compassion. "You should have come to me earlier," he said. "There's a chance I could have healed your pain."

Sheriff Daniels was approaching with his handcuffs at the ready. "All right," he interrupted. "Let's get this over with."

"I need a minute more," Mulder begged.

But Samuel Hartley was already standing, holding his hands behind him. He seemed eager to be on his way.

"I'm afraid I can't help you now," he told Mulder. "My gift is gone."

Mulder stared as the cuffs were put on. Samuel's hands were both bloodied. His wounds looked almost like the stigmata of Christ.

The sheriff and the deputy hustled Samuel roughly toward the door as they were reading him his rights.

The young man paused just before going out.

"I'll tell you, Mr. Mulder," he called back. "God watches his flock. He gives you signs every day. Open your heart, and He just might open your eyes."

Mulder was silent.

Scully sat down at the table, watching her partner, concerned. "How do you think he does it?" she asked.

Mulder shook his head. "I don't know."

He stared at the door until it closed behind the two lawmen and their young prisoner.

Chapter Five

"Given his exemplary record," the defense attorney proposed, "and the highly circumstantial nature of this case, I ask that my client be released on his own recognizance, without bail."

The judge nodded gravely. He seemed to agree that the defendant was no threat.

The spectators whispered among themselves, agreeing.

Even the district attorney seemed to agree.

Curiously, it was the defendant who disagreed.

All through his lawyer's plea, Samuel Hartley shook his head. When she finished speaking, he sprang to his feet.

"Judge!" he cried. "Letting me go is not a good idea!"

The defendant's father, Reverend Hartley, stood up and shouted in dismay: "Samuel! What are you saying?"

"Order in the court!" bellowed the judge, banging his gavel.

Samuel looked worn and pale from his night in jail. He still had a black eye. His clothes were torn and dirty.

He pointed his finger at the judge. "Judge, if you let me go, the next disaster is going to be on your head!"

Everyone in the courtroom gasped—except for Mulder and Scully, who sat quietly watching from the spectators' gallery.

Samuel pointed to the front row, where Reverend Hartley sat with Leonard Vance, the man in black. Even in the courtroom, Vance wore his black hat, gloves, and dark glasses.

Bang! The judge brought down his gavel. The courtroom was quiet.

"Enough!" ordered the judge. "This is not your pulpit, young man. This is a court of law. Understood?"

His eyes locked with the eyes of Samuel

Hartley. It was Samuel who looked away first.

"Yes, sir."

Samuel sat down, and the prosecutor rose to address the court.

"Your honor, in spite of the defendant's avowed guilt, we see no reason to burden the county with his maintenance until trial."

Samuel was ready to stand up and protest again. His attorney held him back with a stern look.

The prosecutor continued: "But we do request a minimum bail of one hundred thousand dollars."

The judge swatted at a fly as he looked at Samuel's attorney.

"Bail is set at one hundred thousand dollars," declared the judge. "Which sum is to be deposited directly into the clerk's probation account, until such time as . . ."

The judge swatted at another fly. But this one didn't go away.

The judge looked down and saw that it wasn't a fly after all. It was much bigger. It was a locust, as big as a grasshopper.

It crawled up the sleeve of his robe. The judge brushed it off, but there was another one.

And another, and another!

The judge looked down and saw locusts swarming on his bench. Hundreds of them. They seemed to be falling out of thin air.

Thousands of them!

"My God, what is this?" the judge yelled. Brushing insects from his hair and off his face.

The court reporter threw down her machine and batted wildly at her hair and clothes.

A guard jumped as he reached for his gun—and found the handle crawling with insects.

Locusts. Thousands of them.

Creeping, crawling, they covered the walls and the floor. Dry wings buzzing, they filled the air.

Mulder and Scully both rose to their feet, swatting at the locusts that crawled over their shoes.

Mulder knocked them off his tie.

Scully brushed a handful out of her hair.

The air was black with buzzing insects. The bailiff ran to shut the window—but it was already shut. *Where did they come from?* Mulder wondered.

Samuel Hartley knew—or thought he knew.

He stood, arms outstretched, his face and hands crawling with insects.

"How much more is it going to take till you BELIEVE?" he implored the fleeing spectators. "Can't you SEE with your own eyes what's HAPPENING? The Lord Himself is TESTIFYING against me!"

No one was listening. Panic gripped the court as the spectators stampeded for the door, shaking locusts from their hair and their clothing, crunching them under their feet.

"Mulder, let's get out of here!" Scully shouted, grabbing her partner's arm.

Mulder followed Scully toward the door. His eyes were locked on Samuel Hartley, who was standing alone in the front, shouting at the fleeing people.

"Does a serpent have to BITE you before you understand?" Samuel cried.

Sheriff Daniels stood by the door. He alone seemed calm and unconcerned. A few locusts crawled across his uniform, but he didn't even bother to brush them off.

Leonard Vance and Reverend Hartley were walking out of the courtroom.

The reverend stopped when he saw the sheriff. The two men locked eyes for a moment—a look filled with hatred. Neither spoke.

Then they both left the courtroom, along with the fleeing crowd.

Chapter Six

It looked like a monster, with its muscular legs, huge jaws, and segmented eyes.

But that was under a magnifying glass.

Scully studied the insect for a few moments, then picked it up with the tweezers and dropped it into a specimen jar. She screwed the lid tight.

Evidence, she thought. *But evidence of what?*

Mulder was at the door. His motel room was next to hers, and since the door was unlocked, he walked in without knocking and sat down on the bed.

Mulder was reading aloud from the Gideon Bible he had found in his room.

"And the locusts covered the face of the whole earth, so that the land was darkened . . ."

"Come on, Mulder," Scully said, turning to face him. "A few thousand grasshoppers hardly constitute a biblical plague."

Mulder shrugged.

"Besides which," she added, "we're in farm country here. This area is an agricultural smorgasbord for this type of infestation."

"Sure, in a cornfield," Mulder observed. "But what we witnessed today happened in the middle of a courtroom, with closed windows and doors."

"So what's next?" Scully joked. "The slaying of the firstborn?"

Mulder didn't answer. He just sat on the edge of the bed, facing her, the Bible in one hand. In the other he held a thick manila folder.

Scully's voice softened. "Mulder, is this about what Samuel said last night in the bar? About your sister?"

Mulder had lost his sister when he was twelve years old. He claimed he had seen her kidnapped by strangers . . . aliens . . . in a bright light. This unexplained tragedy was at the root of his fascination with the X-Files. Instead of answering Scully's question, Mulder handed her the manila folder that he had brought into the room.

"I had these patient records sent over from Kenwood County Hospital," he explained. "These are all physician-documented cases of patients who went to Samuel after conventional treatments failed."

"So?" Scully took the folder reluctantly.

"Take a look."

Scully flipped through the files, reading aloud: "Spontanous remission of metastatic cancer . . . regenerated nerve growth after post-trauma paraplegia—"

Mulder interrupted her. "I've encountered dozens of psychic healers in the X-Files," he remarked. "But I've never seen anything like this."

"Meaning?"

"I think the kid is for real."

Scully looked up, startled. This was the last thing she wanted to hear.

She closed the folder and handed it back.

"I admit it's intriguing," she agreed. "But, Mulder, there's a whole library of medical literature dealing with unexplained cures."

Mulder was undaunted. He paced the floor nervously. "Western medicine treats the human body in biochemical terms," he began. "But the body can also be treated as an electromagnetic system—"

"And your theory," Scully interrupted, cutting to the chase, "is that if Samuel can repair this energy field to heal, then maybe he can destroy it to kill."

"Why not?"

Scully considered this. She shrugged. "Okay, say you're right. Suppose Samuel *can* kill with a touch. It still doesn't answer the primary question, which is—*Why?* Why would he want to kill these people?"

Mulder shrugged. "You heard him, Scully. He says he's 'muddied the water of his faith.'"

Before Mulder could finish there was a knock at the door.

Mulder looked at Scully, then opened the door.

He saw a black hat, black coat, dark glasses—and hideously scarred skin as white as a fish's belly.

Leonard Vance bowed slightly. "If you're available, the reverend would like to see you," he announced.

Both agents picked up their coats and followed him out the door.

Chapter Seven

The Reverend Hartley's Miracle Ministry had paid off in worldly goods. Hartley's "miracle mansion" was almost as big as Graceland, Elvis's famous Memphis home.

The long, curved driveway led between two rows of stately oaks. The front of the house was decorated with huge white columns.

Six Cadillacs were parked in the drive, all in a line. A valet was waxing them, one by one.

A seventh Cadillac pulled up and Leonard Vance got out, followed by Mulder and Scully.

Vance led the two FBI agents into the house. They walked up a wide staircase to a large, elegantly decorated office with windows overlooking the front lawn.

Reverend Hartley sat behind his desk. He rose to greet Mulder and Scully. With a wave of his hand, he sent Vance away.

The scarred man backed out of the room, closing the door behind him.

"I've been under a great deal of stress lately," Hartley confessed. "I hope you'll find it in your hearts to forgive me for my rudeness earlier."

Scully and Mulder looked at him.

"Why did you want to see us?" Mulder asked abruptly.

Hartley looked at the agents. Finally, he spoke up. "I need your help."

Mulder's response was cold. "Samuel is being tried for murder. I think what you need is a good lawyer."

"Samuel is innocent!" protested Hartley.

"What makes you so sure?" Mulder asked.

"Because . . ." Hartley stammered lamely, "because he's my son!"

"Somehow I don't think that argument will work on the jury," said Mulder. "And Samuel's confession won't help much either."

"That confession is meaningless!" Hartley insisted. He looked from Mulder to Scully, his eyes pleading. "You have to understand," he sighed. "Samuel is a very complicated young man."

"In what way?" Scully asked.

"He feels things like no one else," Hartley began. "He feels the suffering of others. He has such sensitivity to others, especially to their pain. To Samuel, a pinprick becomes a gaping wound."

"Are you saying he takes on their guilt as well?" Mulder interrupted.

Hartley didn't answer him directly. "His special power comes from his ability to feel," he continued. "But some people are afraid of his power. And in their fear, they seek to destroy him."

"You mean Sheriff Daniels," Scully prompted.

Hartley nodded. "Among others."

The preacher paused, as if wondering how

much he could afford to reveal. Then he added, "It's no secret that Daniels has been trying to shut me down since the day I first pitched my tent, ten years ago."

"He seems to think your ministry is a fraud," Scully told him.

"That man has no faith, Agent Scully!" Reverend Hartley exploded. "He is a faithless, bitter man. His poor wife suffers from a most painful arthritis. Her fingers are twisted like bitter roots. Yet he keeps Samuel from ministering to her."

Scully was careful to keep her face a blank. "In the light of recent events, I can't say I blame him."

Hartley shook his head, his brow furrowed in pain. "I don't know how those poor people died. I can't explain what happened. Which is why I'm asking you to be there tonight. So you can see for yourself Samuel doing God's work. How about it—will you come?"

"I don't see why not," said Scully. "What do you think, Mulder? Mulder?"

But Mulder wasn't listening. Through the window, he had just glimpsed a strange vision.

On the lawn below stood a girl in a red dress.

A very young girl. A very red dress.

A dress just like his sister had worn, so long ago . . .

She was just standing on the wide lawn.

"Mulder!" Scully repeated.

"Excuse me," he muttered.

Leaving the baffled Scully behind with Reverend Hartley, Mulder bolted out of the office and down the stairs, taking two steps at a time.

He burst out the front door, onto the steps. Blinking in the bright sunshine, he scanned the lawn.

It was empty.

"Where did she go?" he asked the man waxing the Cadillacs in the drive.

"Who?"

"The little girl in the red dress."

The man looked at Mulder quizzically. "There's no little girl around here."

Mulder felt something—a chill on the back of his neck. He looked up and saw Samuel Hartley, staring down at him from an upstairs window.

"Mulder?"

He turned and saw Scully, stepping out onto the porch.

"What is it, Mulder?" she wanted to know.

"A girl . . ."

"Mulder, what are you talking about?" Scully asked.

"A little girl," Mulder answered, still shaken. "But now she's gone."

He looked back to the window where he had seen Samuel watching.

The window was empty. Samuel, too, was gone.

Chapter Eight

"Help yourself!"

Under the black hat and dark glasses, Leonard Vance's scarred face was creased in what passed for a smile.

He stood just inside the entrance to the Miracle Ministry tent, beside a table filled with paper cups and liter bottles of Coke and Pepsi.

Volunteers were pouring refreshments for the worshippers as they filed into the tent, eager to see the young miracle maker they had heard so much about.

"Help yourself!" Vance called out as he handed cups of cola to the crowd. "Let the folks in the wheelchairs through. That's right! Come right on up front. Don't be shy! The Good Lord helps those who help themselves!"

Vance moved through the crowd toward

one of the wheelchairs, which held an attractive young woman in her thirties.

An older couple was walking behind, pushing the chair.

"Welcome to the Miracle Ministry," said Vance, handing a paper cup of cola to the woman in the chair. "Did you all come to see Samuel tonight?"

The woman in the wheelchair nodded stiffly.

The older woman answered for her. "Yes. My daughter was afraid he wasn't going to be here. The papers—"

"Don't pay no nevermind to what you read in the papers!" Leonard Vance assured them. "God's work will be done! Young Samuel is here tonight, ready to cast out the devil and heal the sick."

The older man bent down and placed a hand on his daughter's shoulder. "Did you hear that, honey?"

"Will he be able to see me?" asked the woman in the wheelchair. She looked pleadingly into Leonard Vance's face. If his hideous appearance repulsed or frightened her, she was careful not to show it.

"I'll tell you what," Vance said. "I'll try and put in a special word. What's your name, dear?"

The woman's voice was soft and fluttery. "Margaret Hohman."

"And we're her parents," added the older woman who pushed the chair.

"Margaret, you wait right here," Vance told her. "I'm going to see about getting you a front-row seat."

He patted her hand reassuringly, and she smiled as he moved off into the crowd.

Backstage, Reverend Hartley was also smiling. He was beaming with fatherly pride as he straightened Samuel's collar.

Samuel tried to shrug him away, but the preacher was not to be deterred.

"I can't go out there," he said. "Not after what's happened."

"God tests the faith in us all, son," said Reverend Hartley. "And because He's chosen you to act in His likeness, He's given you the toughest test of all. He is testing your faith in yourself. Do not forsake your gift, Samuel."

"Oh, man!" Samuel groaned, exasperated.

But Reverend Hartley went on smoothly: "I'm a preacher, son. That's my gift. But all the preaching in the world can never equal even one small miracle, Samuel, in consolidating the hope and faith of these people."

Leonard Vance appeared backstage, and Hartley took his hand and drew him over to stand beside Samuel.

"Let this man whose life you saved bear witness tonight, Samuel. Let him bear witness to your healing power."

Samuel looked at Vance. The burned man was silent, his eyes hidden behind his dark glasses. He reached out and touched Samuel's shoulder reassuringly.

"They're waiting for you, Samuel," he said.

Under the big tent the organ was playing and the speakers were blaring.

The seats were already filled with the

young, the old, the black, the white, the rich, the poor.

Some were crying. Others were laughing.

Some were clapping their hands. Others were stomping their feet.

All were waiting for the miracles to begin.

The front two rows were filled with wheelchairs. One of them belonged to Margaret Hohman. Behind and between the wheelchairs, more believers stood leaning on their crutches. Their eyes were filled with pain, even as their faces shone with hope.

Sheriff Daniels and his deputy stood just inside the entrance. The deputy was tapping his foot to the music.

The sheriff scowled at him and he stopped.

Scully and Mulder came in with the last of the crowd. "Let's get a seat," Scully whispered.

No sooner had the two FBI agents sat down than a collection plate was passed to them, overflowing with money.

Scully passed it on. "Apparently miracles don't come cheap," she whispered to Mulder.

"Hallelujah!"

A roar went up from the crowd as Reverend Hartley appeared on stage, looking splendid in a white linen suit. He held a microphone in one hand and a Bible in the other. His rings flashed and his hair gleamed.

"Thank you! God bless you! Yes! Hallelujah!"

The crowd quieted down.

"God is HERE tonight," Reverend Hartley boomed, his voice picking up its hypnotic cadence. "I can FEEL his presence! Oh YES!"

The crowd responded eagerly, "Yes! Yes!"

"And he's here to HEAL!" shouted Reverend Hartley. "Oh YES!"

The crowd was on its feet, those who could stand. Others were waving their crutches in the air. The people in the wheelchairs lifted their arms.

Reverend Hartley pranced up and down the stage, waving the microphone as he spoke. He carried it before him like a burning brand.

"There's a man here I'd like to INTRO-

DUCE," he went on. "A man who has SEEN the face of GOD, but who was not READY to go to that great place that has been PRE-PARED for us ABOVE. No, sir. God had WORK for this brother to do right HERE. Oh, YES!"

"Oh, yes!" echoed the congregation.

"I stand here as WITNESS to the glory of this man's life. He is a modern LAZARUS. I SAW this man come back from death's dark DOMINION, yes!"

"Yes!" The crowd sighed and swayed.

"He stands here tonight as a living TES-TAMENT to God's miraculous LOVE. Yes!"

"Yes!" bellowed the crowd.

Leonard Vance stepped out of the shadows, onto the brightly lit stage. He seemed a creature half made of shadow himself.

"Ladies and gentlemen, brothers and sisters," announced Reverend Hartley. "I give you Leonard VANCE!"

Vance bowed, letting the applause and hallelujahs wash over him.

But he did not remove his hat or his sunglasses.

Reverend Hartley handed him the microphone.

Vance's voice was quieter than Hartley's. People leaned forward in their seats, straining to hear.

"As it says in John, chapter three: 'No man can do these miracles unless God be with him.' That man, to whom I owe my life, is Samuel Hartley. He was but a boy when he saved me. And he is here tonight, as a young man, to heal you! To cleanse you! To touch you with the Lord's healing grace."

The crowd started cheering, and Samuel appeared on stage. The applause turned to rhythmic clapping and stomping.

"Yes! Yes! Hallelujah!"

Mulder and Scully were watching, fascinated, when something caught Mulder's eye.

He turned and looked across the tent, through the crowd.

It was a girl. A little girl.

In a red dress.

She was looking straight at Mulder. He got out of his seat and started through the aisle, toward her.

"Mulder!" Scully called out.

"I'll be right back . . ."

And he was gone, into the crowd.

At the front of the tent, Samuel had stepped off the stage. He was moving across the front row.

The people in the wheelchairs waited for him, their eyes closed, their hands raised as if in triumph.

As he moved down the row, Samuel touched each person on the forehead.

Each person's smile widened.

"Have faith," Samuel said. "Have hope. Be healed."

Mulder slipped through the wildly clapping crowd, looking for the little girl he had seen.

He saw Sheriff Daniels, scanning the crowd with a mean look on his face. But no little girl.

He saw the deputy, tapping his foot, but no little girl.

He saw Scully, looking puzzled.

But no little girl.

He saw Reverend Hartley and Leonard Vance, standing on the stage, leading the chanting, cheering crowd.

He saw Samuel, moving down the row of wheelchairs, laying his hands on each hopeful crippled worshipper.

But no girl.

Mulder bent down and looked under the chair legs. Was that a flash of red?

He heard a scream.

The chanting and the cheering stopped.

But the screaming continued, growing louder and louder.

Scully also heard the screaming.

She leaped from her seat and pushed her

way through the crowd toward the front of the tent.

Samuel Hartley was standing over Margaret Hohman, the woman in the wheelchair Vance had placed in the front row.

She was having convulsions, thrashing horribly in her wheelchair, gulping for air.

Her mother was screaming while her father tried desperately to help her.

Samuel looked on helplessly, his hands clenched into fists at his side.

Leonard Vance and Reverend Hartley stood behind him on the stage, no longer leading the chants but looking on, horrified.

"Stand back!" shouted Reverend Hartley. "Everybody remain calm. Give the woman some air!"

Scully pushed through the crowd and knelt by the wheelchair. "Please," she told them. "I'm a doctor!"

The father and mother backed away so that Scully could get a better look at their daughter.

What she saw was even worse than she

expected. Margaret Hohman was no longer gasping for air. Her eyes were wide open and her head had fallen to one side. She was turning blue.

"Somebody call an ambulance!" Scully yelled.

She looked up and saw Mulder, pushing through the crowd toward her. Behind him she saw Sheriff Daniels, grimly satisfied now that everyone's worst fears were being realized.

Samuel backed away until he stood between his father and Leonard Vance, who took his arms and hurried him off the stage.

Mulder knelt by Scully's side as Scully took Margaret Hohman's pulse.

She looked up at the horrified parents, and then at her partner.

"She's dead," Scully said in a soft voice.

Chapter Nine

It was a quiet night at the Kenwood County Hospital. Quiet inside, that is.

Outside, television cameras and newspaper photographers were gathering. They turned their lights and cameras on a crowd of protesters holding candles, who stood on either side of the main entrance doors under the sign that read: QUIET PLEASE! MAIN ENTRANCE.

It was Reverend Hartley's congregation, but Hartley was nowhere to be seen. Leonard Vance stood at the front of the crowd. He was dressed in black—as usual—pleading in a loud voice.

"Desecrate the body," he declared, "and you SLAY the soul. Let the poor woman's body remain intact. Let the temple be not defiled!"

"Amen," said the crowd.

"Amen, hell," whispered a TV cameraman who was lighting the scene for the eleven o'clock news. "We haven't seen the last of this."

Upstairs, in the second-floor waiting room, Margaret Hohman's mother sat in a shabby orange chair. She was quietly weeping, overcome by the worst sorrow a mother can know—the grief of outliving her child.

The voices from the demonstration below carried into the waiting room: "Believe . . . temple . . . amen . . . sacred . . . amen . . . vessel . . ."

Margaret Hohman's father showed no emotion at all. His hard features were composed into a mask of loss and resignation.

He stood with Mulder and Scully at the other end of the waiting room, where his wife couldn't hear them.

"I know Reverend Hartley is trying to pressure you," Scully said. "But this is the third death linked to the Miracle Ministry. We need your help."

Mr. Hohman listened impassively. He spread his hands in a gesture of helplessness.

"Reverend Hartley says that an autopsy is against Scripture."

Scully silenced her partner with a glance, and changed her tactics. "What illness did your daughter suffer from, Mr. Hohman?"

"She had multiple sclerosis."

"Had she ever had a seizure before this?"

"Not to my knowledge."

"I'm a doctor myself," Scully informed him. "And I think that the seizure she suffered is indicative of some kind of embolism or aneurism. Perhaps even poisoning."

Mr. Hohman looked even more confused. "The boy only touched her forehead," he protested.

Scully nodded. "I know. But are you going to be content to bury her without knowing the true cause of death? Without knowing whether there was foul play involved?"

"No," he remarked, turning toward his wife.

She was crumpled over in her chair, her body racked with silent sobs.

"No," repeated Mr. Hohman to Scully. "Give me a moment, please."

Scully and Mulder stepped aside as he walked over to his wife, knelt beside her, and put his arms around her.

Mulder motioned to Scully with a nod. They moved into the corridor, out of earshot.

"Do you think the boy really did it?" Mulder asked.

"No."

"And why not?"

Scully looked at the sorrowful couple. "I was raised a Catholic, Mulder. I have a certain familiarity with the Scripture."

"And?"

"And God never lets the devil steal the show."

Mulder smiled appreciatively. "You must have liked *The Exorcist*."

"One of my favorite movies."

Scully suddenly turned serious. She had

learned long ago that the best way to get the truth out of Mulder was to ambush him. "Who was it you were pursuing in the crowd tonight?"

Mulder was evasive. "I thought—I saw someone I know."

Scully saw right through him. "The boy has you going, doesn't he?"

"What do you mean?"

"You know what I mean, Mulder. In the bar, Samuel mentioned your sister. The bright light, the . . . alien abduction. Is it your sister you keep thinking you see?"

Mulder gave it up. "I've seen her twice now."

"Maybe you just want to see her."

Mulder moved away, offended. "I'm not delusional, Scully."

Scully was not about to quit. "Don't discount the power of suggestion, Mulder. A healer's greatest magic lies in the patient's willingness to believe. Imagine a miracle and you're halfway there. We learned that in med school."

"Imagination?" Mulder repeated, scornfully. "You think this is what Margaret Hohman *imagined*? Is this what her parents were *imagining*?"

"Sssshhhhh," Scully cautioned. "Here he comes."

Hohman looked as stern and straight as a Bible Belt fenceline. Scully feared the worst. If he turned them down, they were out of luck. Without the autopsy, how could they ever determine the cause of death?

But Hohman surprised her. "My wife and I, we're going to go along with your investigation," he told Scully.

Chapter Ten

Twenty minutes later, Scully was in scrubs. After a little fast-talking and some federal string pulling, she managed to have herself approved to perform the autopsy. It hadn't taken much. The county coroner was glad to have the pressure taken off of him.

The morgue was in the hospital basement. A row of stainless steel drawers in one wall held the bodies.

All but one, which lay on a cold steel table, covered with a sheet. Margaret Hohman.

The morgue was frigid. Mulder stood shivering, watching while Scully sharpened the long autopsy scalpel on a Carborundum rod.

It was a little creepy—especially at midnight in the morgue.

"Ready?" Scully asked.

Scully switched on her tape recorder and placed it beside the body.

"Eleven twenty-one P.M., March seventh," she said as she pulled back the sheet.

Margaret Hohman's eyes were wide open. Scully closed them.

"The autopsy subject's name is Margaret Hohman. Female. Caucasian. One hundred and seven pounds. We begin our incision on the . . ."

In spite of himself, Mulder looked away.

As a federal agent he had seen death in all its forms. But this, the deliberate and methodical dissection of the body of a young woman, was one of the worst.

He could hear the faint sound of the knife as it sliced through cold flesh.

A little more than an hour later, Mulder stood leaning against the wall of stainless steel drawers.

It was over. Scully was washing something in the sink. Something pink.

"Mulder, take a look at this."

"Do I have to?"

Scully held up a bright pink globe of tissue. At first, Mulder thought it was a brain.

"Lesions on the lungs," Scully said. "I'm finding them throughout the pulmonary and cardiovascular system. There is also a lot of damage to the mucous membranes."

"Meaning what?"

"Meaning it looks like Margaret Hohman died of cellular hypoxia. Lack of oxygen to the cells."

"Caused by?"

Scully shrugged. "My guess is ingestion or injection of potassium or sodium cyanide. Maybe arsenic."

Mulder's eyes widened.

"I won't know exactly until I run a toxicology screen on her."

"How soon will that be?"

"The labs won't open till morning," Scully said. Looking up, she saw Mulder gathering his coat. "Wait a minute. Mulder, where in the world are you going this time?"

He was already halfway out the door.

"See who you can push to get it done," he called back.

Mulder stopped just inside the front door to the hospital. He expected the lights and TV cameras to be long gone. But even though it was after midnight, Leonard Vance was still preaching to his small army of the faithful.

Reverend Hartley had joined the party. His lime-green Cadillac was idling at the curb.

Mulder stepped out the door, trying to look inconspicuous. No such luck. When the TV and newspaper reporters saw him, they swarmed.

"Sir! Sir!"

"Excuse me," Mulder muttered, trying to push through them to get to his car. It was no use.

"You're with the FBI?" A reporter shoved a microphone into his face.

"Yes."

"Is it true that an autopsy was performed on Margaret Hohman?"

"Yes. It was just completed a few moments ago."

"Can you give us a definitive answer about the cause of death?"

"Not at this time."

"Will there be an investigation?"

"That's what we'll be recommending to the Kenwood County sheriff's office. Now if you'll excuse me . . ."

He elbowed his way through the sea of reporters until he reached the curb. There was his gray rental car.

And there were Reverend Hartley and Leonard Vance—waiting by the curb.

"You've got some evidence that Samuel's innocent, don't you?" Hartley demanded.

Mulder got into the car and started it before answering. He looked up at Reverend Hartley. The love and concern he saw in the preacher's tired eyes looked real.

"Maybe," Mulder replied as he pulled away.

Chapter Eleven

Jails are like hospitals: places where no one wants to be. The difference is that hospitals are quiet, even in the daytime. Jails are noisy—especially at night.

The Kenwood County Jail was an old-fashioned prison of stone walls and steel bars. Every time a door was opened, the noise rang through the corridors. Each time a toilet flushed, every prisoner heard it.

It was almost two in the morning when the rattling of keys echoed through the main cell block.

Old men and young, white men and black, guilty and innocent, all opened their eyes. They were curious to see who was coming into their dark, barred little world.

All but one.

Samuel Hartley lay stretched out on his bunk with his eyes tightly closed—either sound asleep, or feigning sleep. Whatever the world had to offer him, he didn't want any part of it.

"Samuel."

He opened his eyes just enough to see two figures standing at the bars. One was the jailer.

The other, the visitor, spoke.

"Samuel. It's Agent Mulder. From the FBI."

"Yeah?" Samuel closed his eyes again. "What do you want?"

"I want to talk to you. Would you rather your attorney were present?"

"Whatever," Samuel replied wearily. "No."

The jailer opened the cell door and Mulder stepped in.

The door closed behind him with a sharp, brutal *clang*.

"I've got a call in to Sheriff Daniels," Mulder informed him. "He's on his way down here now."

Samuel Hartley sat up on the bunk, rubbing his eyes.

"What in the world for?"

"I'm asking him to release you."

"Why are you doing this?!" Samuel groaned. "Release me? You were there! You saw it for yourself."

"Did you poison Margaret Hohman?" Mulder asked in a low, calm voice.

Samuel looked at him, confused. "What do you mean? Poison her?"

"Did you poison Margaret Hohman using either potassium or sodium cyanide? Because that's what killed her."

Samuel was speechless.

Mulder dropped his voice.

"You're innocent, Samuel. Unless you had a hand in administering the poison to her. And, quite frankly, I don't think you did."

Samuel groaned and lay back on his bunk. He looked like a man who had just been condemned, not exonerated.

"Whatever the cause, Mr. Mulder, I'm responsible!"

"Come off it!" Mulder shot back. "This is a question of law. The evidence is going to be presented at your arraignment tomorrow.

Habeas corpus law is going to force them to release you anyway, so you might as well get a good night's sleep at home."

"A good night's sleep!" Samuel laughed bitterly. With his hollow eyes and pale, drawn face, he looked like a man who hadn't slept in months. He closed his eyes and turned over to face the stone wall of his jail cell.

"Just leave me alone, okay?"

Mulder was exasperated. "If you believe the punishment for your sins is the deaths of those people, that's your business. But I know—"

"Stop it!" Samuel cried out. "The Lord has testified against me, Mr. Mulder. His wrath is my righteous rebuke."

Mulder shook his head in hopeless frustration. "I can't refute your biblical rhetoric, Samuel. But the law will find you innocent."

There was no response.

Mulder sat down on the bunk beside Samuel. "The other day you said you could see my pain. What do you see now?"

Samuel lifted his head and looked into Mulder's eyes. Then he looked away.

"I don't see anything. I'm blind."

"I don't believe you."

"Why would you doubt me?"

"Because—I've seen her, Samuel. It *was* her, wasn't it?"

"Your sister?"

Mulder nodded. "You made her appear to me, didn't you?"

Instead of answering, Samuel closed his eyes.

"Look at me!" Mulder said angrily.

"I am very tired, Mr. Mulder," Samuel replied without opening his eyes.

"Is she alive?" Mulder demanded. "Is that what I'm supposed to believe? Or was it—just a trick?"

Samuel lifted his head and opened his eyes slightly. He smiled. It was a cold, chilling smile.

"You mean a trick of the devil, Mr. Mulder?"

Mulder shivered, in spite of himself. He had looked for hope in Samuel Hartley, but what he saw was something even darker than despair.

He started to speak, but decided against it. Instead, he called back over his shoulder.

"Jailer!"

Chapter Twelve

Sheriff Daniels was waiting in the jailer's office when Mulder came out of the cell block.

He stiffened when he saw the FBI agent. "I see I'm a little late for this ball," he said with a sneer. "What exactly are you doing here at two in the morning?"

"I called you down here to ask you to release the boy," Mulder replied.

Sheriff Daniels raised an eyebrow in mock surprise. "On what pretense?"

"His innocence."

"You're a little out of your depth here, aren't you, Agent Mulder? This may be Hicksville to you, but we do try to abide by the legal system."

Mulder sighed. "I'm not going to argue

with you, Sheriff. Samuel Hartley seems determined to stay here in jail anyway."

Daniels nodded. "And what does that tell you?"

"It tells me you are determined to have him charged," Mulder answered, "while your real homicide suspect is still at large."

Without waiting for a response, Mulder brushed past the sheriff and left the jail.

The sheriff watched Mulder get into his car and drive away. Then he turned to the jailer and, without a word, pointed toward the cell block where Samuel was held. Then he drew his finger across his neck—the same signal he had given the backhoe operator.

The jailer nodded.

It was clearly an order.

Moments later, the jailer appeared at the door to Samuel's cell.

He was not alone.

Two men were with him. Big men, who stood behind him in the shadows.

"Got some company for you, Sam."

The jailer's keys rattled noisily as he unlocked the door. The two men walked into the cell.

The cell door clanged shut behind them with a nightmarish sound.

Samuel Hartley stood calmly to face his two visitors. It was almost as if he had been expecting them.

The jailer was halfway down the corridor before he heard the first blows.

CRACK! BLAP! BLAM!

It was an ugly sound. And there were no cries of pain or protest.

The other inmates lay awake, listening. One of them stood at the bars of his cell as the jailer passed.

"What are you staring at?" the jailer threatened. He rattled his keys menacingly.

The inmate lay back down and closed his eyes.

BLAM! CRACK!

The sounds of the beating continued as the jailer left the cell block and went into his office.

He closed the door.

CRACK! BAM!

He could still hear it, the sound of metal on flesh.

He turned on the radio, to a country music station.

He turned up the volume to drown out the sounds of the beating.

There. He sat down and put his feet on the desk and lit a cigarette.

That was better.

Chapter Thirteen

Sheriff Daniels's cruiser sat parked in the driveway of a small, unassuming-looking house.

Inside, his wife, Lillian, was sitting in her wheelchair, reading the Bible. She was turning the pages with her twisted fingers when the doorbell rang.

She closed her Bible and started for the door, rolling painfully slowly in her wheelchair. It was hard for her to get up speed.

Sheriff Daniels strode out of the kitchen, wiping his hands on a dishtowel. He pushed past his wife impatiently.

"I got it, I got it," he grunted.

He opened the door. It was his deputy, Dennis Tyson.

Tyson removed his hat nervously and nodded. "Ma'am. Sheriff."

"How are you, Dennis?" Lillian Daniels asked sweetly.

"Just fine, ma'am. Except . . ."

His eyes evaded hers and found the eyes of Sheriff Daniels.

"Well, what is it?" Daniels snapped.

"Except that we had . . . an incident down at the jail."

The sheriff's voice was deadpan as he mocked the deputy. "What sort of incident would that be, Tyson?"

"The preacher boy," replied the deputy. "He's dead."

Mrs. Daniels opened her mouth in a silent scream of horror. The Bible slid off her lap and thudded to the floor.

Sheriff Daniels lifted his hat off the peg on the wall and followed his deputy out the door without a word.

The door slammed shut behind them.

Lillian Daniels sat alone and cried. She had

always hoped that someday the sheriff would relent, and let her go to the tent meeting to be healed.

Now that hope was gone forever.

The crowd that had gathered outside the jail was quiet. They stood back, watching, as the men from the county coroner's office rolled the body out. It was zipped into a black plastic body bag.

Mulder followed the gurney through the crowd. He watched as it was loaded into the coroner's van, then turned to look for his partner.

He found Scully talking with Sheriff Daniels.

"He was alone in his cell when Mulder left him last night," she said. "How could this have happened?"

Sheriff Daniels shrugged. "The boy picked a fight," he told her. "Got into it with a couple of good ol' boys we had picked up for drunk driving."

"Good ol' boys?" Mulder asked. "We're

talking about a murder here, Sheriff."

"Samuel took some mean blows to the head," the sheriff replied, as if that explained everything. "Died before the ambulance even got to the jail."

Scully touched Mulder's arm. Reverend Hartley had just arrived and was approaching across the courthouse lawn. He walked with long strides, like an avenging angel.

His face was streaked with tears, and his mouth was twisted in cold fury.

He pointed a long finger at Sheriff Daniels. "Samuel's blood is spilled, and it's all over you!"

Leonard Vance was right behind him. He laid his hand on the preacher's shoulder. "Reverend—" he said in a soft voice, trying to turn the preacher away.

Hartley ignored him. He stared into the sheriff's face. "How much longer can you hide behind that badge before the truth is revealed?" he demanded.

Sheriff Daniels spat expertly into the grass. "I have work to do," he said, turning his back.

He walked off, leaving Reverend Hartley standing between Scully and Mulder, shaking with grief and anger.

Scully touched the preacher's arm. "Reverend Hartley," she said, "we are sorry for your loss."

Hartley's face sagged. The rage was gone, leaving only sorrow. He looked old and defeated.

"That boy was blessed," he groaned in a low voice. "He never hurt a soul."

Leonard Vance's gloved hand appeared again on the preacher's shoulder.

"Come on, now, Reverend," he urged gently. "Our friends will be finding out about Samuel sooner rather than later. And it's probably best if they hear it from you."

Hartley nodded in agreement and followed Vance toward his Cadillac.

Scully looked at Mulder, who was deep in thought.

"You have that look on your face, Mulder," she remarked.

"What look is that?"

"The kind you have when you've forgot your keys and you're trying to figure out how to get back in the house."

Mulder looked around. The crowd was gone. Even the sheriff and his deputy had left. Mulder looked toward the empty courthouse, and then toward his partner.

"Come on, Scully."

"Where we going?"

"Hunting," he replied.

Mulder and Scully entered the courtroom where Samuel Hartley had been arraigned.

The empty courtroom was quiet, but in her imagination Scully could still hear—and see—the swarm of locusts that had filled the room only days ago. It was creepy.

"Exactly what are we trying to find?" she asked as she followed Mulder toward the judge's bench.

"Clues," he answered cryptically.

"Oh," she replied, just as cryptically.

The courtroom was dark. Shadows bisected the dim light that came through the tall, dusty windows.

Crunch.

Mulder looked down. The floor was still litttered with dead insects. He bent down and picked one up.

Then he looked up, to the ventilation grille directly above the judge's bench.

The grille was open.

Scully followed his eyes, from the dead insects to the open vent. "What does it mean?" she wondered.

"Let's find out," said Mulder.

Moments later, thanks to a helpful janitor, they were on the roof. The sky was darkening to the east.

"Storm coming up," Scully noted, pointing to the dark clouds on the horizon.

Lightning flashed through the sky, like a threat.

Mulder wasn't watching. He was leaning over the air-conditioning unit.

The intake grille was loose, and littered with small slivers that looked like wood chips.

He picked one up. "Scully!"

She tore her eyes away from the gathering storm and joined him.

Mulder squeezed the small gray sliver, and juice ran out.

"Potato."

He flicked it away, and brushed his hands on his pants. Then he pointed at the others in the vent.

"Someone left a food trail through the vent system," he observed. "Leading straight into the courtroom."

He pointed toward the inlet pipe.

"They dumped the locusts in there. Instant plague."

Scully bent over and looked down the pipe.

"But the locusts—where did they come from?"

"Biological supply houses will hatch them on special order," Mulder told her. "For farms, universities, research facilities, all sorts of stuff. It shouldn't be too hard to find out who ordered some. Then we'll know who set this up."

CRRRRAAAAAAACK!

Lightning split the sky—too close for comfort. The wind was picking up. "So you think whoever it was—is also behind the murders?" she asked.

Mulder didn't answer. He didn't hear her. He was already running to avoid the first huge raindrops.

Chapter Fourteen

Lightning split open the night, and the sudden brilliant flash illuminated the many-columned facade of Reverend Hartley's "miracle mansion."

The house was dark. The doors were locked. The Cadillacs were lined up in the driveway, their windows rolled up to keep out the pouring rain.

Inside the mansion, everything was still. Only the thunder and the drumming of the rain could be heard. The only light came from outside the windows, when the lightning flashes split the sky.

CRRRRAAAAAAACK!

On the second floor, Reverend Hartley slept in his gigantic, luxurious master bedroom.

He had taken several sleeping pills, and even a stiff shot of bourbon—his first in years—to ease the pain of his grief and rage.

The drumming rain drowned out his snores.

In a smaller bedroom down the hall, Leonard Vance tossed and turned. His restlessness seemed to mimic the storm outside.

The storm ripped the leaves from the trees.

Vance kicked the blankets off the bed.

He groaned, thrashing like a man trapped in a nightmare.

Without his black hat, his cheap wig looked almost ridiculous.

Without his dark glasses, his face looked even more hideous than ever.

Without his gloves, his hands were disfigured strips of twisted skin.

His lips were thin lines of scar tissue.

He had no eyebrows, no eyelashes.

CRRRRAAAAAAACK!

Leonard Vance suddenly opened his eyes wide.

Someone was in his room, standing at the foot of his bed, staring at him.

It looked like . . . but it couldn't be.

"You're dead!" Vance groaned. "They killed you!"

The face of Samuel Hartley was as pale and white as the face of Leonard Vance. His body seemed as insubstantial as a dream.

Yet there he was, dressed in the same blue shirt and white slacks he had worn at the last tent meeting.

"Dead!" croaked Vance.

"I *was* dead," Samuel said in a soft, accusing voice. "But here I am."

"No!"

Vance scrambled out of his bed and backed up against the wall.

CRRRRAAAAAAACK!

When the lightning flashed, the room was empty. There was no one there.

Then the darkness returned and Vance could see him clearly.

Samuel stepped toward Vance. Slowly, relentlessly.

One step, two.

"Get away!" screamed Vance.

"Why?" Samuel asked in a cold, emotionless voice. "Why did you betray me?"

Vance charged at his tormentor, filled with sudden rage. He picked up his cane from the head of the bed. Wielding it like a sword, he slashed at Samuel.

It went right through him.

Vance slashed again, backing away.

CRRRRAAAAAAACK!

There was another flash of lightning, and Samuel—the apparition, the ghost?—was gone.

Leonard Vance wiped his brow and breathed a sigh of relief.

A dream. It must have been a dream.

"You murdered those people . . ."

Vance stiffened. The voice was behind him now.

He wheeled around, and there, in the darkness—

Samuel. Again.

Approaching slowly, step by step. Across the creaking floor.

Vance swung the cane once more, but it slashed harmlessly through thin air. Samuel kept approaching, closer and closer.

"They came to be healed," Samuel intoned accusingly. "They came to be healed by me. And you murdered them."

Vance threw the cane. It went right through Samuel. It hit the wall and clattered across the floor.

"Why?" Samuel beseeched him. "Why did you betray me, after I gave you back your life."

"Life?" Leonard Vance thrust out his grotesque, disfigured hands. "You call this—life?"

He ripped the wig off his head, revealing his scarred scalp. "And this?"

Trembling with humiliation and rage, he began to sob. He covered his lashless eyes with his scarred hands.

Samuel shook his head sadly and advanced another step.

CRRRRAAAAAAACK!

Chapter Fifteen

Reverend Hartley was having a dream.

Bells. Church bells, tolling.

Wedding bells? Funeral bells?

No, they were chimes.

The doorbell!

He opened his eyes. A glance at the window told him that the storm was still raging. A glance at the clock told him it was the middle of the night.

Where was Vance? He usually got the door.

The doorbell chimed again.

"Who could that be, at this hour?" Reverend Hartley muttered. He stumbled out of bed, pulling his robe around him.

CRRRRAAAAAAACK!

A flash of lightning lit up the windows as

Hartley walked down the stairs and opened the front door.

Sheriff Daniels stood on the porch, dripping wet. With him were Mulder and Scully.

"You?" Reverend Hartley asked Daniels. "What do *you* want?"

Without bothering to answer, Sheriff Daniels stepped inside.

Mulder and Scully followed.

The sheriff reached into his jacket and pulled out a folded piece of paper. He handed it to Reverend Hartley.

"We have a warrant for the arrest of Leonard Vance. Where is he?"

"You must be mistaken," Hartley answered. With trembling hands he started to unfold the paper.

Scully saved him the trouble. "Afraid not, Reverend," she said. "We traced a pesticide order to him from a chemical company in Knoxville. Cyanogen bromide—a cyanide derivative."

"You're telling me Leonard *poisoned* those people?"

Scully nodded. Mulder watched silently, saying nothing.

Sheriff Daniels was impatient. He took his handcuffs from his belt, put one foot on the stairs, and barked, "Where is he?"

Reverend Hartley led the way to the upstairs room where Leonard Vance slept.

He knocked. No answer.

He opened the door and followed the three law enforcement officers into the bedroom.

Leonard Vance lay on the bed, covered by a sheet.

"Get some clothes on, Vance," ordered Sheriff Daniels, holding out the handcuffs. "You're coming with us. We're placing you under arrest."

There was no response

Scully crossed the room to the bedside. She could see that Vance was sweating.

He was shaking. His hands lay on top of the sheet, trembling.

Scully took his hand to check his pulse.

Vance opened his lashless eyes. "I betrayed him," he said in a parched whisper.

Scully saw an empty glass on the bedside table. Picking it up, she smelled it and wrinkled her nose. "Cyanide. No way to tell how much he ingested."

"I'll call an ambulance," said Mulder, turning toward the door, where Reverend Hartley stood in shocked silence.

"No time," Scully answered. "We'll have to take him to the hospital ourselves."

She began wrapping the blankets around Vance, who now began to shiver violently.

"Why didn't he let me die?" Vance raved, his head nodding wildly from side to side on the sweat-stained pillow. "Beware of false prophets! They will come to you in sheep's clothing, but inside they are ravenous wolves! That's what I thought he was. A false prophet!"

"Who?" asked Mulder, leaning down.

"Who else would bring me back looking— like this?" cried Vance, holding his twisted hands to his scarred face.

"But I was blinded by my vanity," he groaned. Vance began to weep. "And I betrayed him."

Mulder bent down closer so he could hear what Vance was saying. "Who are you talking about?" he demanded. "You betrayed who?"

"Samuel," Vance rasped. "He was here."

Sheriff Daniels stiffened and looked behind him, into the dark corners of the room. He seemed frightened by what he had heard. "The man's delirious!" he insisted.

It was more a wish than an observation.

Leonard Vance reached out for Reverend Hartley's hand. Hartley tried to step back, but it was too late.

Vance caught his hand and pulled him toward the bed.

"He was here, Reverend," Vance whispered. "Right in this room!"

Sheriff Daniels shuffled uncomfortably, the handcuffs rattling in his hand. "Nonsense!" he declared.

Vance pulled Hartley down to the bed. "Samuel was here . . . and he forgave me!"

Before Reverend Hartley could respond, Vance jerked once, twice—

CRRRRAAAAAAACK!

A flash of lightning tore open the night.

Leonard Vance's eyes rolled back in his head.

Scully reached for his wrist to feel his pulse. But it was a futile gesture, and she knew it. The man was dead.

Daniels put the handcuffs away.

Mulder stared out the window, into the pouring rain—and perhaps beyond.

Chapter Sixteen

"Rather than simply killing Samuel," Scully typed on her laptop computer, "Vance contrived to kill the ministry's faith in him."

It was morning. The investigation was over, the federal part of it at least.

While Scully waited for Mulder to finish packing, she sat at the desk in her motel room, typing their report.

"We have conclusive evidence connecting Leonard Vance to both the courtroom infestation and to the poisoning deaths of the three members of the Miracle Ministry.

"Vance's obsession outlived Samuel, however," Scully noted. "His conscience haunted him until he became delusional. He thought he saw Samuel's ghost and took his own life—thereby effectively ending our investigation.

"In light of this information," Scully typed, "it is highly doubtful that there have been any miracles in Kenwood, Tennessee."

Scully shut down her computer and packed the last of her clothes.

While his partner typed their report, Mulder finished putting his things in his suitcase. The last thing he packed, as always, was a small framed picture.

Mulder took the picture off the bedside table and wiped the glass, even though it wasn't dusty.

It was a photograph of a little girl in a print dress.

The same little girl whom Mulder had caught glimpses of over the past few days.

His sister, Samantha.

Putting aside his own faint hopes for a miracle, Mulder tucked the photograph in the suitcase and closed it carefully.

As he was snapping the locks shut, the phone rang.

x x x

A minute later there was a knock on Scully's door. When she answered it, Mulder stood in the doorway.

"Scully, I just got a call from Sheriff Daniels. It seems that Samuel's body is missing from the morgue."

Chapter Seventeen

Less than half an hour later, Mulder and Scully stood in the morgue in the basement of the Kenwood County Hospital.

The room was cold.

Some of the stainless steel drawers had white tags. Each of these contained a human body.

Or was supposed to.

While Scully watched, Mulder pulled open the drawer tagged H534.

The drawer slid open smoothly on its rollers, as if eager to cooperate with the FBI.

It was empty.

"Any witnesses?" Mulder wanted to know.

"One," answered Deputy Tyson. He stood with Sheriff Daniels by the door. "The night nurse who made the report, Beatrice Salinger.

She's waiting upstairs in the nurses' lounge. Says she wants to talk to us."

"She saw someone take the body?" Mulder asked.

Tyson hesitated. "Not exactly."

"Talk sense, Deputy!" Sheriff Daniels snapped. "Did she or didn't she?"

"She didn't, uh, exactly see anybody take the body," Tyson replied.

"What, then?" barked the sheriff scornfully. "What *exactly* did she see?"

"She, uh . . ." Deputy Tyson reddened with embarrassment. "She, uh, she claims she saw Samuel walking out all by himself."

The sheriff and the two FBI agents turned to face the deputy, who stammered:

"I know! Sounds crazy, I know. But that's what she told me, I swear!"

"Let's talk to the nurse," Scully suggested. She led the way out the door.

Mulder paused when he saw Sheriff Daniels hanging back. The big man looked shaken.

"You coming, Sheriff?"

Swallowing hard and nodding, Daniels followed.

The nurses' lounge was as warm and cozy as the morgue had been cold and sterile.

Beatrice Salinger was a woman in her mid-thirties whose friendly face was sprinkled with freckles. Her tired eyes and worn hands testified to years of experience with the sick and dying.

Not the kind to tell ghost stories, Scully thought as she listened.

"I was drinking my coffee," Salinger began. "Going over the night orders for my ward, seven south . . . when he walked right by me. His face was all black-and-blue. Samuel."

"And you're sure it was him?" Mulder asked.

The nurse nodded. "At first I thought my eyes were playing tricks, which can happen on the graveyard shift. So I got up to look again."

"And?" Scully asked.

"I lost him. Lost him around a corner, like he just vanished. So I went to check the morgue."

Mulder and Scully, Daniels and Tyson, all were silent. Their eyes were on the nurse.

"You saw yourselves what I found. His body was gone."

Sheriff Daniels shook his head violently as he edged toward the door.

"This is insane," he exclaimed. "I refuse to listen to any more of this woman's crazy talk!"

He opened the door to leave the lounge.

Nurse Salinger turned in her chair and faced him. "I'm not the only one who saw him, Sheriff Daniels. So I know I'm not crazy. Other people saw him, too."

Looking as if he had been slugged, the sheriff left and closed the door behind him.

Nurse Salinger turned back toward the deputy and the two FBI agents.

"I'm not crazy," she calmly asserted. She looked from Mulder to Scully and back to Mulder. She ventured a slight smile. "It was Samuel."

Chapter Eighteen

It was late afternoon before Sheriff Daniels made it home. Perhaps, as he said later at his trial, he had been simply driving around aimlessly. Perhaps he had been thinking. Perhaps he had been praying, although he later claimed he neither believed nor prayed.

It was late afternoon when he found himself parking in his drive, walking up to the house he had shared with his wife for twenty years.

He found her waiting for him, her wheelchair parked in the center of the living room. Her eyes were ablaze with something between fury and pain.

In her lap, which usually held a Bible, there was a newspaper.

"It isn't true, is it?" she wailed. Her twisted fingers crumpled the newspaper.

MURDERED FAITH HEALER RISES FROM DEAD!
DOZENS WITNESS "MIRACLE"

The sheriff didn't answer. He took off his gun belt and hung it by the door.

He hung his hat over it.

"This is just a big lie to sell newspapers, isn't it, Maurice?"

Sheriff Daniels didn't answer.

His wife's voice took on an awful tone of bitter irony as she shouted:

"The boy was just a fake, like you always said, wasn't he, Maurice? That's why you wouldn't let me go to him and be healed, right?"

She started crying quietly.

He sat down without answering and stared out the window.

It was getting dark.

It was almost a relief to Sheriff Daniels when he heard a car pull into the driveway. His wife was still crying quietly.

He stood up slowly when the doorball rang. "I'll get it," he sighed. It was the first time he had spoken since he had come home.

He opened the door. He wasn't surprised to see that it was Tyson, his deputy.

"Sir," Tyson reported. "I don't rightly know how to say this but . . ."

"Speak up, Deputy."

"I'm going to have to ask you to come with me."

Daniels nodded. He reached for his hat and his gun belt hanging by the door.

"The district attorney wants to ask you some questions about Samuel Hartley's death," Tyson continued. "Apparently those good ol' boys implicated the jailer, and he sort of, well, sort of implicated you."

Daniels handed his gun belt to the deputy without being asked. He put on his hat.

"Let's go, then," he said, without a word or glance toward his wife.

The door closed on the quiet sobs of Lillian Daniels.

Her small world had gotten smaller still.

Chapter Nineteen

The Miracle Ministry tent was coming down.

The gray rental car pulled up as workers were sorting the stakes and folding the canvas.

A worker on a tall ladder was taking down the marquee sign.

MIRACLE MINISTRY
COME AS YOU ARE . . .
LEAVE AS YOU ALWAYS WANTED TO BE!

Mulder and Scully got out of the car and watched as two workmen removed the plastic letters from the sign and tossed them into a box.

"Sundays probably won't ever be the same in these parts," Scully mused, interrupting Mulder's thought.

"I wouldn't be so sure," he replied. "The Reverend Hartley may just move on to greener pastures. I have a strong sense that he won't be able to give up the pulpit."

"Even without his son?" asked Scully.

"It might even strengthen his faith. Remember, the boy did rise from the dead."

"Sure," said Scully, smiling wryly. "And I witnessed a biblical plague of locusts. I just hope Reverend Hartley didn't arrange the body-snatching as his miracle of miracles."

"Somehow," said Mulder, "I don't think so."

There was something in his voice Scully had heard before. A note of yearning.

She looked at him sideways. "Well, what exactly *do* you think, Mulder?"

"I think people are looking for miracles, Scully. Maybe so hard that they make themselves see what they want to see."

He stared off into the distance.

After a long moment, Scully said, "We've got a plane to catch. Ready to go?"

"Yeah."

Mulder followed Scully back to the car. He

was just about to get in when he saw something reflected in the window glass. An image.

A young girl.

In a print dress.

He wheeled around, but she was gone. Or maybe she had never been there.

All he saw was the folded tent, the empty sign, the ladder.

Mulder got into the car with his partner and drove off without looking back.